Based on the TV series *Nickelodeon Avatar: The Last Airbender*™ as seen on Nickelodeon®

SIMON SPOTLIGHT

An imprint of Simon & Schuster Children's Publishing Division
1230 Avenue of the Americas, New York, New York 10020
© 2008 Viacom International Inc. All rights reserved. NICKELODEON,
Nickelodeon Avatar: The Last Airbender, and all related titles, logos,
and characters are trademarks of Viacom International Inc.
All rights reserved, including the right of reproduction in whole or in part in any form.
SIMON SPOTLIGHT and colophon are registered
trademarks of Simon & Schuster, Inc.
Manufactured in the United States of America
First Edition
1 2 3 4 5 6 7 8 9 10
ISBN-13: 978-1-4169-5062-2
ISBN-10: 1-4169-5062-1
Library of Congress Catalog Card Number 2007933064

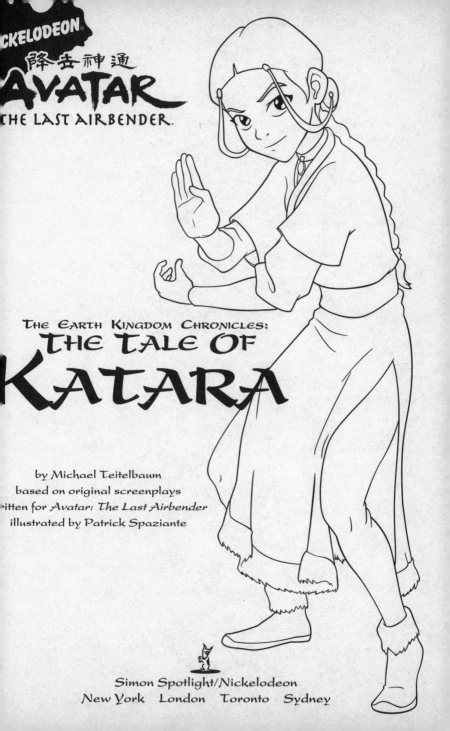

NICKELODEON®

降世神通

AVATAR
THE LAST AIRBENDER

THE EARTH KINGDOM CHRONICLES:
THE TALE OF
KATARA

by Michael Teitelbaum
based on original screenplays
written for Avatar: The Last Airbender
illustrated by Patrick Spaziante

Simon Spotlight/Nickelodeon
New York London Toronto Sydney

Chapter 1

My name is Katara. I'm a Waterbender from the Southern Water Tribe. My brother, Sokka, and I are traveling with Aang, the Avatar; his sky bison, Appa; and his lemur, Momo. I'm teaching Aang Waterbending, but now he has to start mastering Earthbending. He's got to learn all four elements to stop the Fire Nation from taking over the world.

Aang's old friend King Bumi of the Earth Kingdom city of Omashu will be his Earth-bending teacher, so that's where we're heading now. It's time to say good-bye to Pakku, the Waterbending master I met at the North Pole.

As we say our good-byes, Master Pakku hands me a crystal amulet.

"It contains water from the Spirit Oasis. The water has unique properties. Don't lose it."

I promise to keep it safe, and use it for something really important.

As we started traveling, we met a group of singing nomads. "We're heading for Omashu," I explained.

"That's dangerous," Lily, one of the nomads, said. "The Fire Nation is spread out to the coast. You'll be headed right for them."

Hmm. We need to get to Omashu, but I don't want to risk a run-in with the Fire Nation.

"There's a story about a secret pass through the mountains," Chong, another nomad, said.

Then he sang a song about two lovers whose people were at war. They were separated by a mountain, but they used Earthbending to create tunnels so they could meet secretly. It sounds so romantic! I wouldn't mind checking it out, but Aang said no because Appa hates going underground. I guess I'll have to check out the tunnels some other time.

The second we took off, the Fire Nation attacked us! So I'm going to get my wish after all—we're going through the Cave of Two Lovers.

"Secret love cave, let's go," muttered Sokka.

Of course, he had no problem getting all lovey–dovey with Princess Yue. . . . I could tease him about that . . . but nah, I'll let it go for now.

"The legend says that only those who trust in love can make it through the caves," Chong said as we entered.

What does that mean? Trust that love will bring you to the right person, or trust the love you already feel for that person? I wonder if Gran Gran trusted in love, if that's what made her leave Master Pakku and go south. Did she let love lead her to my grandfather instead? I wonder where love will lead me. . . .

What's that sound? It's getting louder! Now I hear wings flapping—wolf–bats! Now Appa's going crazy, slamming into everything—

BOOM! Oh, no! The cave wall's collaps-ing. Can't see. Dust everywhere. AHH! The rock slide's coming toward me!

In a flash Aang grabbed me and flew me just beyond the edge of the rock slide. Phew!

But where are the others? It looks like they're trapped on the other side of a mountain of rocks. "If we try to dig through, we're going to cause the whole thing to cave in."

"Sokka will find a way out," Aang says.

"Let's hope we can too."

Okay, so, Aang, Appa, and I are making our way through the tunnels. Hey, there's a huge round door—maybe it's a way out!

"It's a tomb," Aang announces. "It must be the two lovers from the legend."

8

Of course! They must've been buried here together. "Look, it says 'Love is brightest in the dark.' What do you think that means?"

Aang shrugs. "How are we going to find our way out of these tunnels?"

I guess that means he's not answering my question. It would be nice if sometimes he would talk about his feelings WITHOUT me having to drag them out of him. Oh, well, I guess we should focus on getting out of here. They say that love is brightest in the dark . . . I wonder if . . . no. But what if it works? Or what if it causes . . . some confusion? We'll never know until we try, right? "I have a crazy idea."

"What?"

Oh, no. What if this is the worst idea ever? And I'm just caught up in some romantic dream with all this talk about the two lovers and trust—ing in love! He'll think it's stupid. Maybe he'll even laugh at me. "Never mind. It's too crazy."

"Katara, what is it?"

"Well." All right, here goes nothing. "The nomads told us that the curse says we'll be trapped in here forever unless we trust in love."

"Right."

"And next to this picture of the lovers kissing it says 'Love is brightest in the dark.'"

"Where are you going with this?"

Oh, boy. He really doesn't know what I'm getting at? Or wait, maybe he does but he doesn't want to embarrass me so he's pre—tending not to. Wait, that's just crazy. This is not SO far—fetched; it IS the Cave of Two Lovers. Just say it. "What if we kissed?"

"Us, kissed?" Aang repeated.

He's stunned; he's numb from the shock. Now things are going to be all weird between us. I knew this was a mistake. "See, that WAS a crazy idea." I have to play it down. "Us kissing. What was I thinking? Can you imagine that?" I guess Aang never thinks about kissing me. Strange, I was almost positive he had, too. Oh, well.

"Yeah, ha. I definitely wouldn't want to kiss you."

I guess he's really NEVER thought about it. That's fine—wait a minute! What? He definitely wouldn't want to kiss ME? It's not like I wanted to kiss HIM. I just suggested it because of that saying. How dare he? Am I so repulsive that he couldn't ever imagine kissing me for any reason? I didn't think it would be so bad . . . but apparently, HE did. Hmph. "Oh, well, I didn't realize that it was such a horrible option."

10

"No, I mean if it was a choice between kissing you and dying, I—"

So, the only way Aang would ever kiss me is if his other option was death! Nice to know he thinks so highly of me. "Well, if I had that choice I'm not sure which one I'd rather do!"

That's it. I'm leaving. No use standing around looking at two lovers' tombs—it's just making me feel worse. They trusted in love and love found them. But what happens when I trust in love? NOTHING, because the person I put my trust in would rather die than kiss me.

Wait a minute, what am I getting so worked up about? I mean, I care about Aang a lot, but it's not like he's my boyfriend or anything. We are just friends. And friends don't kiss, so it's not really fair for me to be mad at him.

Oh, no—our torches are starting to fade. Soon it's going to be pitch-dark in here.

"We're going to run out of light any second now, aren't we?" Aang finally said.

"I think so."

"Then what are we going to do?"

"What can we do?"

What's he doing? It looks like he's moving toward me. He's moving closer and closer. Is he trying to kiss me? I thought he didn't want—oops, the torches just went out! It's totally dark; I can't even make out where he is. . . . Okay, Katara, just close your eyes and go with it. . . .

Whoa! Lights just went on! They're forming a path across the ceiling! Huh, I guess love really is brightest in the dark!

"They're crystals," Aang said. "They must only light up in the dark."

"Of course. That's how the two lovers in the legend found each other. They put out their lights and followed the crystals."

We made it. We're out!

And there's Sokka, Momo, and the nomads! Looks like they're riding badger—moles.

"How'd you get out?" Sokka called out.

"Just like the legend says, we let love lead the way," Aang said.

Hmm, maybe love did lead the way. I'm still not exactly sure what that means, or what Aang means by saying it, but I guess we'll have to leave that for another time.

"Really?" Sokka said. "We let huge ferocious beasts lead our way."

So, now we're heading toward Omashu's front gate. The last time we were here, Sokka and I spent most of our time enclosed in creeping crystals—hope this visit is better than that!

Whoa, what's going on? Something's terribly wrong here. There's a huge Fire Nation flag hanging from the city's main wall. This is worse than we ever imagined. Omashu is in the hands of the Fire Nation!

Chapter 2

"I can't believe it," Aang said, hanging his head. "Omashu always seemed untouchable."

It's so unfair! The Fire Nation just keeps taking people Aang cares about—first the Air Nomads, now King Bumi. "This is horrible, but we have to move on."

"No. I'm going in to find Bumi."

I knew it. I knew he wouldn't stay focused. "Aang, let's talk about this. There are other people who can teach you Earthbending."

"This isn't about finding a teacher; it's about finding my friend," Aang said sadly.

Well, I'm not leaving Aang. If he's

determined to go in, we're going in with him.

We snuck into the city through a disgusting sewer pipe. Poor Sokka got covered by the mold and filth in the tunnel and ended up with little round marks all over his skin from tiny creatures called purple pentapi. But the pentapus marks helped us fool Fire Nation soldiers into thinking that Sokka had a contagious disease called pentapox! They stayed clear of us after hearing that. We were free to roam the city.

What's that rumbling? It sounds like another rock slide. AHHH! Huge boulders are rolling down Omashu's mail chutes—and they're heading right for that family!

Aang quickly Airbended the boulders away from the family. Close call, though.

"The resistance!" shouted the woman.

The what?

Now the teenage girl is hurling flying daggers at us! What is she doing that for? Aang just saved her life. It doesn't make any sense— AHHH! We're falling through the ground!

Where are we? It looks like some kind of

underground cavern. And who are all these people in uniform? Oh, the resistance!

"Is King Bumi with you guys?" Aang asked.

"Of course not!" a resistance member shouted angrily. "On the day of the invasion King Bumi surrendered!"

This doesn't make any sense. Why would Bumi surrender? Aang looks devastated. . . .

"It doesn't matter now," said the man who turned out to be the resistance leader. "Fighting the Fire Nation is the only path to freedom, and freedom is worth giving anything for."

"You could just leave Omashu," Aang suggested. "You're outnumbered, you can't win. Retreat now and live to fight another day," he said before leaving to find Bumi.

Sometimes I forget that he's the Avatar. It's funny, most of the time I just feel like I have to protect him from the Fire Nation, but actually he's the one who's protecting us. But we need to find him an Earthbending teacher, and if it isn't going to be Bumi, we might have a long search ahead of us.

So, we're not fighting; but how are we going to evacuate the thousands of citizens of

Omashu with the Fire Nation's permission?

"You're all about to come down with a nasty case of pentapox!" Sokka announced.

That's it! It's a perfect plan. I knew we could count on Sokka. He may be goofy sometimes, but he's a master of schemes and solutions for all sorts of sticky situations.

By putting purple pentapus marks on all the Earth Kingdom citizens, they looked like they had some terrible disease. The Fire Nation governor ordered all the "sick" people to leave the city. So, we gathered on a hillside outside the city to plan our next move, but King Bumi is still nowhere to be seen. I guess I just have to trust that Aang will find his way back to us once he has Bumi. Aang IS the Avatar—I'm sure he'll be fine . . .

Oh, look! There he is with Bumi's pet, Flopsie. But no Bumi. Aang looks so upset.

"We've got a problem," the resistance leader said suddenly.

Well, looks like we picked up an extra person—the Fire Nation governor's baby son! He's so cute! But how did he get mixed up with us? We can't continue on with him—we'll have to face them again.

It seems like the governor wants to trade his son for King Bumi! So Aang, Sokka, Appa, Momo, and I are heading back into the city for the trade.

Okay, there they are. There are three girls. That one I recognize! She was with that family we saw. They must be Fire Nation, she's the governor's daughter. But I have no idea who the others are. And where's Bumi?

What's that? It looks like a metal cage. It's dropping down from above.

Thank goodness he's still alive! Let's just get this over with. I will be sad to give up this little fire baby, though. They're still so cute before they know how to fight.

"The deal's off!" yelled the governor's daughter suddenly.

What happened? Now Bumi's cage is shooting back up into the sky.

"Bumi, no!" Aang cried as he flew into the air, landing on Bumi's cage.

"We've got to get the baby out of here!" I shouted, handing the little guy to Sokka.

I've got to help distract these girls so Aang can get a clean getaway. Oh, no! One of the Firebenders is following him!

Well, time to focus my energies on the girls who remain. Take that! An ice shield should halt her daggers—yup. Now let's just encase her arm in ice—whoa, what's that? Who's that behind me? The third girl—she's poking me with her fingers! What does she think that'll do?

I'll just Waterbend this puddle at her and— wait, what's going on? Nothing happens when I try to Waterbend! That girl did something to me! She took away my bending ability!

"How are you going to fight without your bending?" snarled the girl with the flying daggers, preparing to fling one at me.

I'm completely powerless! There's absolutely nothing I can do to stop her!

BOING! What's that? YES! It's Sokka's boomerang, knocking the daggers from her hand!

"I seem to manage just fine without bending," he said as he reached down and pulled me up onto Appa's back.

My brother the warrior, here in the nick of

time. He also returned the Fire Nation baby. Now we're flying toward Aang, who is still without Bumi.

"Let's go," Aang said. "I'll explain later."

Well, looks like we're finally leaving Omashu. At least we're back on track to find Aang an Earthbending teacher. I still can't believe that that girl somehow blocked me from bending. What if I never get my bending back?

As Appa soared above the Earth Kingdom, my bending ability slowly returned. I can't believe how vulnerable I was to that attack without my bending. I guess we're all vulnerable sometimes. I'm just glad it's back.

I wonder where we should fly to next to find an Earthbending teacher. Aand said Bumi told him to find a teacher who waits and listens.

"Hey, Aang!" cried Sokka. "Why are you taking us down?"

We are flying down for some reason. But there's nothing down there but a big swamp. . . .

"I think the swamp is calling to me," Aang said. "Bumi told me that to learn Earthbending I would have to wait and listen. And now I'm actually hearing the Earth."

"I don't know, Aang. There's something ominous about this place."

Then, out of nowhere, a giant tornado started zooming toward us. The funnel slammed right into us, sending me tumbling to the swamp below. Aang and Sokka landed nearby. But Appa and Momo are nowhere to be found.

We looked for them, but then it got dark, and now it's time to set up camp for the night. . . .

AHH! Something's grabbing my leg! Am I still dreaming? No, whatever it is, it's real! Swamp vines—they're dragging me into a thick mist. Got to cut myself free with a water whip.

Phew! I'm free. But where is everyone else? "Aang! Sokka!"

Nothing. They can't hear me. I'm lost. What if I never find them? What if we never find Appa? Wait, who's that? There's a woman over there. "Hello? Can you help me?"

Why won't she answer me? I'll just get a little closer and—no, it can't be. How can it be her? "Mom? Mom! Is it you?" I don't believe it. I've missed her so much. And now when I need her most, when I'm lost and alone she comes back to me. It will be so amazing to have her back! All the things I can ask her about now— she can come with us so I never have to leave her side again. I can ask her what it means to trust in love. She'll definitely know! "Mom, I—"

What? How can this be? She's gone. It doesn't make sense. I saw her with my own eyes. She was right there! There's something really strange about this place. She was so real, but it was never her. It was just my imagination. And now I miss her more than ever.

After I collected myself, I went looking for Aang and Sokka. They had visions too. And it turns out that the Swamp Monster is actually just a Waterbender whose job it is to protect the swamp. Anyway, we finally found Appa and Momo, too, and now we're back en route to finding Aang an Earthbending teacher. We're severely behind schedule at this point, but I guess there really isn't anything we could do to fix that. We just have to hope that we find him a teacher who waits and listens soon.

Chapter 3

We're finally somewhere that Aang has a chance at finding an Earthbending teacher, the town of Gaoling. Aang said he overheard two guys talking about an Earthbending competition, so he went to find out where it is.

"Excuse me, but where is this Earthbending competition, exactly?" Aang asked politely.

"It's in the town of Nunya," one guy answered. "Nunya business."

Sometimes boys are so . . . idiotic. It's not that hard to just tell us where it is—besides, the joke wasn't that funny. I mean, Sokka laughed at it, but that's not saying much. Aang looks so defeated. I'll take care of this.

"Hey, strong guys, wait up!"

Look at them—they're so narcissistic! I bet they think I'm impressed by their muscles. Ha! What girl would be impressed by guys who get their kicks out of making fun of other people? While their arrogance keeps them distracted, I'll just get my skin of water out and—

THWACK! Ha! Head to toe icicles— horizontal icicles, that is. "So, where's that Earthbending competition again?"

"Hey, Aang," I shouted out, leaving my handiwork behind and rejoining the gang. "You ready to find an Earthbending teacher? Because we're going to Earth Rumble Six."

"How'd you get them to tell you?"

"Oh . . . a girl has her ways." They deserved every last piece of ice I sent their way. Really, to go picking on poor Aang like that. I hope they learned their lesson.

Some of the best Earthbenders in the world are competing at Earth Rumble Six. So we came to watch, hoping one of the competitors will be the teacher Aang has been waiting for.

"Welcome to Earth Rumble Six, forty fighters vying for a shot at becoming the Earthbending champion!"

I know I'm here to help Aang find a teacher, but there are a million places I'd rather be. This is just going to be another display of mindless male aggression. At least Waterbending and Airbending are all about the element. "This is just going to be a bunch of guys chucking rocks at one another, isn't it?"

"That's what I paid for," Sokka said.

One by one the big bruisers keep slamming rocks into one another. It seems like there isn't even any thought involved. Okay, there's one guy left standing now. He's a hulk who calls himself the Boulder.

"And now," Xin Fu, the announcer, bellowed, "welcome your champion, the Blind Bandit!"

Whoa! The champ is a girl. And she's half the size of the rest of these brutes. She calls herself the Blind Bandit, huh? "She can't really be blind. It's just part of her character, right?"

"I think she is," Aang said.

She's remarkable! It's like she can sense where the Boulder is. It's hard to believe she's blind. Whoa! She just slammed the Boulder across the arena, and all she did was press her foot against the ground and thrust her hands forward. "How did she do that?"

"She waited . . . and listened," Aang said with a big smile on his face.

Then Xin Fu announced, "I'm offering this sack of gold pieces to anyone who can defeat the Blind Bandit! Who dares to face her?"

"I will!" Aang cried, jumping into the ring.

What's he doing? He doesn't want to fight her! Oh, he thinks she's the Earthbending teacher he's looking for. He wants to talk— only, she doesn't seem too interested in talking! She just flung a boulder at him! He just knocked her from the ring—Aang beat her!

She's leaving. She just opened a doorway in the wall and stormed through it. Aang looks so disappointed.

"Way to go, champ!" Sokka said, running to Xin Fu and grabbing the sack of gold.

Sometimes Sokka can be so . . . thick!

After we left the arena, we went searching for the Blind Bandit. We discovered that she's a member of the Beifong family, the richest family in town. Then we found her house. It's more like an estate with really high walls, beautiful gardens, and a gigantic mansion.

We've decided to climb over the wall and slip into the gardens.

FOOM! The ground just rose up beneath me! I'm flying through the air! OOMPH! Ouch! This bush doesn't feel so good. . . .

"What are you doing here, Twinkle Toes?"

It's her. She's obviously not thrilled that we snuck into her home. I can't really blame her.

"Aang is the Avatar," I explained. "And if he doesn't master Earthbending soon he won't be able to defeat the Fire Lord. He needs you to be his teacher."

"Not my problem," the Blind Bandit said.

Not her problem? She may think she's safe behind these walls, but no one is safe from the Fire Nation—and that's everyone's problem.

Well, our first attempt at talking to her didn't go so well, but Aang's brilliant idea of pre-senting himself as the Avatar to her father has gotten us back in for good.

Toph's parents—Toph is the Blind Bandit's real name—have no idea that she's this amazing Earthbender. She pretends she's a helpless little blind girl. Seems very strange, and kind of—I don't know—sad, if you ask me. She has all this strength and power when it comes to standing up to those Earthbenders, but none when it comes to her parents.

After dinner Aang and Toph went for a walk. Hopefully they're talking about Earthbending. Actually, it's getting kind of late. I think I'll go and check things out, just in case.

What's that on the ground? Oh, no! It's a ransom note. It says: "If you want to see your daughter again, bring five hundred gold pieces to the arena." It's signed by Xin Fu and the Boulder.

We all hurried to the arena, where we found Toph and Aang trapped in metal cages.

"Here's your money," Sokka said. "Now let them go."

Xin Fu released Toph.

"What about Aang?" I asked.

"I think the Fire Nation will pay a hefty price for the Avatar," Xin Fu replied.

Uh-oh. All the Earthbenders from the

tournament are here too. . . . There are too many of them. . . . We can't do this alone.

"Toph, we need an Earthbender. We need you."

"My daughter is blind and helpless," her father said. "She cannot help you."

What's it going to be, Toph? Are you going to just let these guys deliver Aang to the Fire Nation? Or will you help us?

"Yes. I can."

I've never seen such incredible bending. Toph single-handedly wiped out every Earthbender in the arena! Then we freed Aang.

Now we're back at the Beifong house. I can't believe how Toph's father is reacting. Now I understand why she kept it a secret.

"From now on you will be guarded twenty-four hours a day!" he said. "It's for your own good."

Why is he so stubborn? His daughter is unbelievably talented and he treats her like she's completely helpless. It's so unfair. She should be allowed to be who she is, and to teach Aang, not be held like a prisoner. Now we have to find someone else to teach Aang. He's going to be so disappointed—again.

As we prepared to leave, Aang explained that Toph had told him that she "sees" by feeling the vibrations of moving things and figuring out where they are. She waits and listens, just like King Bumi said. Too bad her father is a fool. Still, I've got to keep Aang's spirits up. I can't let him give up.

"Don't worry, Aang. We'll find you a teacher. There are plenty of amazing Earth-benders out there."

"Not like her."

He's right about that. Now what can I say? Wait, who's that? It's Toph!

"My dad changed his mind," she said. "He told me I was free to see the world."

This is fantastic! Although admittedly, it does sound very odd. Five minutes ago he was ready to lock her up for the rest of her life; suddenly he's ready to set her free? You know what—it's not my business and it's not my problem. I have to worry about Aang. Perhaps Toph will be more than just a teacher . . . Maybe she'll be a friend, too.

Chapter 4

30 We've finally landed and we're setting up camp for the night. I can't wait to go to sleep!

What's Toph doing? We're all setting things up and she's stretched out on her back, relaxing. I can't believe she—okay, Katara, wait, calm down. She's not used to being in a group. She's always been a loner. Just explain to her how we work and I'm sure she'll pitch right in.

"So, Toph, usually when setting up camp we try to divide up the work."

"Hey, don't worry about me," she replied.

Worried? Can she possibly be this clueless? "Actually, some of us fetch water, while others set up the fire pit, or put up the tent."

"Katara, I'm fine," she said impatiently. "I can carry my own weight. I don't need a fire, I already collected my own food, and look"—SWOOSH—"my tent's all set up."

Unbelievable! This is NOT okay; she's part of this group now. She has to pitch in. "That's great for YOU. But we still need to finish—"

"What's the problem here?!"

Now she's giving me attitude! It's time to tell her just how selfish she's being—but wait, Aang needs her. I can't run her off. Just calm down and walk away. "Never mind."

Okay, you're calm; it's time to make peace.

"Hey, Toph, I wanted to apologize for earlier. I think we're all just a little tired and getting on each other's nerves."

"Yeah, you do seem pretty tired."

HMPH! She is just infuriating. She won't admit that she was wrong. She just turns it back on me. "I meant ALL of us were tired!"

I'm so frustrated, I could scream! Now she's slipping into her tent like nothing happened. We might have to travel together, but we don't have to be friends. It's unfortunate, because it would have been nice to have another girl to talk to, even though she's not that girly. But this was her choice, not mine.

I had just fallen asleep when Toph woke us up.

"There's something coming toward us!" she cried. Her hands were pressed against the ground, feeling the vibrations of whatever it was.

So we took off. Now that we're up on Appa, we can see something steaming across the land, chugging out smoke. Is it following us?

Finally, a safe-looking spot to set up camp. Let's see if Toph cares to help this time around.

"See you guys in the morning," said Toph.

I guess that's a no, then. She's sprawling out again, like some kind of princess. "Actually, Toph, can you help us unload?"

"You need me to help unload Sokka's funky-smelling sleeping bag?"

"Well, yeah," I said. "And everything else. You're a part of the team now, and—"

"Look, I didn't ask you to help unload my stuff. I'm carrying my own weight."

Well, I don't care if she IS Aang's teacher—she's got to start acting like part of this team.

"That's not the point. Ever since you joined us, you've been nothing but selfish and unhelpful!"

"Look here, Sugar Queen. I gave up everything I had to teach Aang Earthbending, so don't talk to me about being selfish!"

"Sugar Queen!" How rude! I can't believe her. SHE'S the one who grew up in a rich mansion with two living parents who love her and protect her, and I'M the Sugar Queen? I grew up in ice huts, my mother was captured and my father left to go to war! And I've been fighting the Fire Nation for the past year. What has SHE done? Competing in secret Earthbending competitions doesn't make you tough, sweetheart. Facing a war does. UGH! She is the most maddening person I've ever met. I'm just asking her to do her fair share. She's acting like it's some great imposition and—

Okay, Katara, once again, you're way too wound up. She's not worth it. You know you're not a Sugar Queen, you know how strong and brave you've been. Don't let her tear you down. Just calm down . . . deep breaths.

"That thing is back," Toph called out.

I guess we have bigger problems than

Toph's selfishness. That thing IS following us. Time to head out . . . again.

🪙 🪙 🪙

The tank thing followed us up this cliff. Aang wants to see who they are and what they want. The tank is opening. . . . It looks like three girls, riding on mongoose–dragons. Hey! "It's those three girls from Omashu!"

"We can take them!" Toph announced.

The three riders charged toward us. Toph put up a thick wall of rock to stop them, but one of the girls blasted the wall open with fire that looked like lightning! She is one power–ful bender. We're way too exhausted to fight these girls. Time to get going, again. . . .

🪙 🪙 🪙

"Appa can't keep flying forever," Aang said.

Just then Appa crashed down in a clearing.

"We've put a lot of distance between us and those girls, so let's get some sleep," Sokka said, collapsing to the ground.

"We could have gotten some sleep earlier if Toph didn't have such issues," I pointed out.

"What?!" she shrieked.

Must have hit a nerve.

"All right, everyone's exhausted. Let's just get some rest," Aang said.

"No, I want to hear what Katara has to say. You think I have issues?"

"If you had helped, we could have set up our camp faster and gotten some sleep."

"You're blaming ME for this?" Toph asked in disbelief.

"No, no," Aang chimed in. "She's not blam— ing you."

"Yes, I am blaming her!" And I'm right. This needs to be settled if we're going to be a team.

"Hey, I never asked you for anything," Toph shot back. "I carry my own weight. Besides, if there's anyone to blame, it's Sheddy over here!"

Whoa, she just stepped into one huge mistake. Prepare to hear the fury of Aang.

"You're blaming Appa?" Aang cried.

"He's leaving a trail of fur," Toph explained. "That's how they keep finding us."

Aang is furious, and I don't blame him! If she hadn't been so horrible earlier I would step in and help, but she brought this on herself.

"How dare you blame Appa!" he shouted. "He saved your life three times today! You're always talking about how you carry your own weight, but you don't. Appa does. He carries your weight. He never had a problem flying when it was just the three of us!"

Okay, that was harsh. Did I sound like that?

"I'm out of here," Toph said. Then she picked up her pack and walked away.

She's just going to pack up and leave? That's so typical, only thinking about herself. What about Aang's Earthbending lessons?

"What did I just do?" Aang moaned when he had calmed down. "I just yelled at my Earth—bending teacher and now she's gone."

It's not OUR fault! I mean, she should have helped us, as part of the team! And blaming everything on Appa, well, that's just wrong. I mean, I guess he IS shedding, and it makes sense that that's how they are following us. But she still has no excuse for being so selfish.

Although, I guess I forgot that Toph is really just a kid who left her home and parents behind to travel the world with total strangers. I could have been a bit more sensitive to that. I just kept going on and on about helping set up camp like we always do. But that's the thing:

She's new to the whole WE thing. I should have asked her how SHE does things too, instead of just assuming that she'd fall into whatever routine we already had going. I should have asked her how she was feeling about being away from home instead of yelling at her to set up camp. Oh boy, it IS our fault! "We need to find Toph and apologize."

Aang set off with some of Appa's fur to set up a false trail, just in case those girls in the tank are still following us. Sokka and I headed off to find Toph, but so far we've had no luck.

Hey, there's Aang! He's battling that girl, the lightning Firebender, and someone else. It's . . . PRINCE ZUKO! And there's Zuko's uncle Iroh. And who IS this Firebending girl who can shoot lightning? Time to fight!

Why is the ground shaking? What's hap- pening? Hey, it's knocking the Firebending girl down. But what's making it shake?

"I thought you guys could use a little help," Toph said.

Boy, am I glad to see her! And we can sure use her help right now!

Give it up, Firebending girl. You're surrounded. Even Zuko and Iroh are against
you.

"Well, look at this," she cackled. "Enemies
and traitors working together. I know when I'm
beaten. A princess surrenders with honor."

Princess? She's Zuko's sister?

BOOM! A searing bolt of lightning just
struck Iroh.

Surrender! What a liar! SWOOSH! Take
this water whip. Wait—she disappeared!
What a coward. . . .

Iroh is badly hurt. Zuko looks like he might
even be crying. Zuko is my enemy. But now
I feel sorry for him. It even seemed that for a
moment he was on our side against his sister.
Maybe I can heal his uncle with my Waterbending. "Zuko, I can help."

"Leave!" he screamed, launching a wave of
fire just inches above our heads.

What can I do if he doesn't want my help?
At least everyone else is safe, and Toph is
back. I guess it's time to go.

Chapter 5

The next morning Toph began Aang's Earth-bending lessons.

"Good morning, Sifu Toph!"

"Hey, you never call me Sifu Katara!"

"Well, if you think I should . . ."

What does that mean? Doesn't he think I deserve the title? Maybe he doesn't think I'm a good enough teacher . . . but everything he knows he learned from me! And Toph hasn't taught him one move yet. What do I have to do to make him see that I deserve it too?

Maybe in order to prove that I really am a master, and a teacher, I have to behave like one. Hmm . . . I'm sure after a day of lessons with Toph, he'll realize how lucky he is to have Sifu Katara teaching him Waterbending. . . .

"Maybe if I came at the boulder from a different angle—," Aang suggested.

"No, Aang, that's the problem," Toph said angrily. "You've got to stop thinking like an Airbender. There's no different angle or tricky solution. You've got to face the rock head-on."

Aang looks pretty freaked out. After teaching him for over a year, I know exactly what he does and doesn't respond well to, and yelling and bullying don't work. I think Toph could use some help from Sifu Katara. . . .

"I've been training Aang for a while now, Toph. He really responds well to kind words, praise, encouragement." Exactly, just show them that you know what you're talking about. They'll respect your knowledge.

"Thanks, Katara. I'll try that."

See! It worked. I guess I'll head back to the camp. I'm glad I can make Aang's training easier. And if he realizes what a great teacher I am in the process, well that's fine too!

Okay, so I left Aang and Toph alone for a while, but I'm just too curious. I'm also concerned about how Toph is handling Aang. I have to go back and check in again.

"This time, instead of trying to move a rock, you're going to stop a rock," Toph shouted. "Get in your horse stance!"

I wish she wouldn't yell at him like that. He really does do better with positive encouragement. Now Toph's pointing to a large boulder that's on top of a cliff. Aang's at the bottom.

"I'm going to roll that boulder down at you. If you have the attitude of an Earthbender, you'll stay in your stance and stop the rock."

This is crazy! Aang isn't ready for this. Toph's pushing him too fast, and he could really get hurt. "Sorry, Toph, but are you sure this is the best way to teach Aang Earthbending?"

"I'm glad you said something, Katara. Actually, there is a better way."

See, she listened again. Even Aang is smiling from relief. If I haven't proven myself worthy of the title Sifu Katara by now, then I don't know what will earn it for me. They

41

obviously both respect my teaching abilities. Maybe Toph'll slow down a bit and— What's she doing? She's putting a blindfold over Aang's eyes. What good will THAT do? That is certainly NOT what I implied when I made my comment! She's a real sneak, that Toph.

"Now you'll have to sense the vibrations of the boulder to stop it. Thank you, Katara."

Now she's making fun of me. She thinks I'm meddling, but I only have Aang's best interests in mind. And I still think my methods are better!

"Yeah," Aang said, obviously unhappy.

"Thanks, Katara."

Now Aang's annoyed at me. Why does Toph have to twist everything I say? She is so infuriating. . . . Why does she bother me so much? We're not competing for his attention or anything. Aang and I still have a special connection. He doesn't have to call me Sifu Katara. We're too close for such formal titles.

Boy, here we go. The boulder's rolling. It's huge and it's heading right for him. He's not experienced enough to stop it. This is too advanced. He's going to be crushed!

No, he's leaping out of the way. Phew!

I knew he wasn't ready for this. She really should have listened to me.

"I guess I just panicked," Aang said, removing his blindfold. "I don't know what to say."

"There's nothing to say," Toph yelled, getting in Aang's face. "You blew it. You had perfect form, but when it came right down to it you didn't have the guts. Now, do you have what it takes to face that rock like an Earthbender?"

"No," Aang said sadly. "I don't think I do."

This is terrible. Screaming and humiliating him is no way to teach. All she's doing is breaking his spirit, not making him a better bender. I have to do something.

"Aang, it's no big deal. Take a break, and try again when you're ready. We still have a lot of Waterbending to work on. Okay?"

"Yeah, that sounds good," Aang replied.

"Yeah, whatever!" Toph shouted after us. "Go splash around until you feel better."

She is so insensitive. And she's a horrible teacher! Sifu Toph—ha, what a joke!

"You know this block you're having is only temporary, right?" I told him.

"I don't want to talk about it!" Aang yelled.

"You have to face the issue instead of avoid—ing it. That's the Earthbender way."

"I know I need to face it head—on, like a rock. But I just can't do it and I don't know why!"

I know why. "Aang, if fire and water are opposites, then what's the opposite of air?"

"Earth, I guess."

"And that's why Earthbending is so hard for you; it's your natural opposite. But you'll figure it out. I'm sure of it." He seems calmer. Now for a confidence booster. I'll just fling this reed at and him and—"Quick, cut it in half!

"Excellent, Aang. You have the reflexes of a Waterbending master."

"Thank you, Katara. Sifu Katara."

He's smiling! He seems much better—wait, did he say Sifu Katara? Is he bowing? I really needed to hear that. Now if I could only change Toph's teaching methods . . .

I've spent all day worrying about Aang, I just realized I haven't seen Sokka in hours. "It's almost sundown and Sokka isn't back yet!"

"We'll find him faster if we split up," Aang said. So we headed out to search.

I've had no luck. Now I'm back at camp. What if something happened to him? I hope Sokka's all right. It's almost completely dark.

Wait, what's that? It sounds like Aang and Toph, and they have Sokka! "You found him!"

"Hey, Katara. Look what I can do!" Aang shouted. Then he Earthbended a huge rock.

"You did it! I knew you would!" I knew he had it in him. It was just a matter of time and patience. I guess Toph learned something too.

"You tried positive reinforcement, didn't you?" I whispered to her.

"Yup," she replied. "It worked wonders."

See, I knew it! We're one step closer to defeating the Fire Lord.

After a few weeks of hard work, we decided to take vacations. My choice didn't turn out so well, but we ended up meeting this professor from Ba Sing Se University, who told us about this ancient library somewhere in the desert.

"Do you think they'd have maps or infor— mation about the Fire Nation?" Sokka asked.

"If such maps and information exist, then it is in Wan Shi Tong's library," the professor said.

So, Sokka decided that's where we're going to spend his vacation.

We finally found the library. Aang, Sokka, Momo, and I went inside while Toph stayed outside with Appa. Inside the library, Sokka learned that the darkest day in Fire Nation history is the day of a solar eclipse because there is no sun to fuel their fire. Then we found this calendar that told us when the next solar eclipse would be. That's when we're going to attack the Fire Nation. We had a little trouble getting out of the library, but we made it out just in time!

We're out! Back on the desert sand! Now we can actually celebrate this news! I can't believe it—my brother, the hero! This news is going to change the course of the entire war. It's going to change the history of the world forever! We finally have a plan to win this war, and it's all thanks to Sokka!

"The Fire Nation's in trouble now!" shouted Sokka, giving me a big hug.

"Toph?" Aang said. "Where's Appa?"

Huh, where IS Appa? I don't see him anywhere. And Toph is just sitting there shaking her head. Oh, no, what's happened to Appa?

Chapter 6

Appa's gone! We finally have good news to celebrate, and this happens! I've come to count on him to carry us everywhere and save us when we're in trouble. I don't know what we'll do without him in this desert, in this heat. Poor Aang. Appa's not just a pet or a ride; he's Aang's family, his best friend. This is awful. How many loved ones can one person lose?

"How could you let Sandbenders take Appa?" Aang screamed at Toph.

I guess while we were in the library a group of Sandbenders—Earthbenders who can manipulate sand—captured Appa.

"I couldn't stop them," she cried. "The library was sinking and I was trying to keep it up. I can hardly feel any vibrations in the sand, so I can't see. They snuck up on me and—"

"You just didn't care!" Aang yelled. "You never liked Appa. You wanted him gone!"

Wait, I know Toph has rubbed us all the wrong way at times, but Aang's not being fair. I know he's upset, but yelling at Toph isn't going to bring Appa back. "Aang, stop it! You know Toph did all she could. She saved our lives!"

"I'm going after Appa," Aang announced, opening his glider and taking off.

48

"We'll never make it out of here," Sokka moaned.

Aang's gone, Toph feels horrible, and Sokka is losing hope. I can't let everyone give up. It's not just about us surviving. It's about the survival of the whole world. "We'd better start walking. We're the only people who know about the solar eclipse. We have to get that information to Ba Sing Se."

Sometimes I wish there was someone for me to lean on . . . but this is just the way it is. I have to keep us together. I have to get this information to the Earth King. I just have to.

We're practically out of water. Everyone is hot and exhausted. Still, we have to keep moving. We've got to find a way out of the desert.

There's Aang! He's come back . . . alone. "I'm sorry, Aang. I know it's hard for you, but we need to focus on getting out of here."

"What's the difference?" he replied. "We won't survive without Appa. We all know it."

I can't let his despair make the others lose all hope. "Come on, Aang, we can do this if we work together. Right, Toph?"

"As far as I can feel, we're trapped in a giant bowl of sand pudding. I got nothing."

Sokka is stretched out on his back, staring up at some circling birds.

It's up to me, then. I'm not letting them give up and just sit here waiting for the end! "We are getting out of this desert and we're going to do it together. Aang, get up. Everybody hold hands!"

On we trudged until night began to fall. "I think we should stop for the night."

"Appa!" Aang cried as he looked up.

"Sorry, Aang. It's just a cloud." I really wish it were more than a cloud—a cloud! That means water! "Aang, fly up and bend the water from that cloud into my pouch."

Aang snatched the pouch from my hand impatiently, opened his glider, and flew up toward the cloud. I know he's upset, but really, his behavior isn't fair. No matter, here he is with the pouch. At least now we have water.

Huh, it feels awfully light. "Wow. There's hardly any water in here."

"I'm sorry, okay!" Aang shouted angrily. "It's a desert cloud. I did all I could. What's anyone else doing? What are YOU doing?"

He is so angry, so uncontrolled. I know he's sad about Appa, but it's not like I don't know what it feels like to lose a loved one. He's certainly not going to get through it by alienating the people who are still here for him. If I could wish Appa back here, I'd do it in a second. But I can't.

"I'm trying to keep everyone together."

Just then Toph stubbed her toe on something in the sand. It turned out to be a buried sandsailer, the vehicle Sandbenders use to glide along the desert, using wind power.

"Aang, you can bend a breeze into the sails to make it move. We're going to make it!"

We dug out the sailer and set off across the desert. But we soon ran into some Sandbenders who accused us of stealing their sailer.

"I recognize the voice of one of the Sandbenders," Toph said. "He's the one who stole Appa!"

"Where is he?" Aang shouted at the Sandbenders. "Where's my bison?"

Aang's going crazy! He's blasting the Sandbender's gliders to pieces. I've never seen him so angry. He may actually hurt someone.

"Tell me where he is. Now!" Aang screamed.

"It wasn't me!" the Sandbender cried, obviously frightened by Aang's rage.

"You're the one who said to put a muzzle on him!" Toph said.

"You muzzled Appa?!" Aang yelled.

"I'm sorry. I didn't know it belonged to the Avatar!" the Sandbender admitted. "I traded him to some nomads. He's probably in Ba Sing Se by now. They were going to sell him there."

Aang's eyes are going blank. His tattoos are glowing. Now the wind is whipping up all around him. He's so furious, he's slipping into the Avatar state. His power is unbelievably strong, but completely out of control. It's like a giant tornado is surrounding him, spreading in all directions.

"Run!" Sokka shouted, grabbing Toph and pulling her away from Aang.

No. Not me. I'm not running away from Aang. I'm going right through the tornado funnel. I don't care how dangerous it might be. Aang needs me and I'm not letting him down. Just reach up and—got him! Now he's looking down at me. See, he's coming back down. He just needs to know that I'm here for him. After everything he's done, everything he's meant to me, it's the least I can do. I am not letting go.

There, the wind is calming down. He's coming out of the Avatar state. It's okay, Aang. I'm here. And I'm not going anywhere.

Aang's mood seemed to improve as we made our plans to travel to Ba Sing Se. On a map from the spirit library Sokka found a route along a narrow strip of land called Serpent's Pass. Then we met a family of refugees, including a pregnant woman named Ying who told us about a much safer route, by ferry. Unfortunately the refugee family's passports and tickets were stolen at the ferry port, and it was back to Serpent's Pass. Before we left the ferry port, Sokka ran into Suki, a Kyoshi warrior who we had met earlier in our travels. I think Sokka really likes her. She's here work—ing as a security guard, but decided to come along with us. She must like him, too!

🎴 🎴 🎴

At the entrance to the pass there's a sign. "It says 'Abandon hope.'"

It's so strange. Hope is what's kept me going through the darkest times, like our journey across the desert, and right after my mom passed away. Sometimes hope is all you have.

"The monks used to say that hope is just a distraction," Aang said. "Maybe we do need to abandon it."

"What are you talking about, Aang?"

"Hope isn't going to get us into Ba Sing Se, and it's not going to find Appa. We need to focus on what we're doing right now, and that's getting across this pass."

Aang is usually so positive about things. He's always the one saying that everything's going to work out. I'd hate to think he's lost hope completely. But whatever he needs to do to lead us to Ba Sing Se, I'll support him. And this is just temporary, I'm sure of it. "Okay, Aang. If you say so."

That night at our campsite I found Aang, alone, staring off into the water. He may be telling everyone that he's okay now, but I know him. He's not himself. And he seems to be in total denial about what happened to Appa.

"You know, it's okay to miss Appa. I don't know what's going on with you. In the desert all you cared about was finding him. Now it's like you don't care about him at all."

"You saw what I did out in the desert. I was so angry about losing Appa, I couldn't control myself. I hated feeling like that."

"But now you're not letting yourself feel anything. I know sometimes it hurts more to care, but promise me you won't stop caring."

He's so quiet. I hated seeing him so angry before, but at least he was feeling something. "Come on. You need a hug."

I'm standing here, arms wide open, and he's just standing still.

"Thank you for your concern, Katara," he said, bowing. Then he walked away.

Aang's turning down a hug? And he's being so formal, so cold. It's like he flipped off the switch that allows him to feel, and the sweet, sensitive guy I've come to know and care about so much has just gone away. I guess I'll give him his space for now. It just makes me so sad to see him like this, but we all have to grieve in our own way. He'll come around, I know it.

The next morning we came to a huge body of water. The only way to cross this is if I literally part the water so we can walk through.

"Single file, everyone," I called out.

It seems like it's working—we just have to get to the other side. Okay, we're halfway there. . . . Wait, what's that?

Suddenly the water went black; all the fish are swimming away. . . . AHH! It's a giant serpent. I've never seen anything so gigantic in my life! It's attacking us. I lost our safety bubble. We're about to get soaked—THOOMP!

Phew! Toph Earthbended a huge sand platform and lifted it into the air, above the water. At least everyone is safe. Now Aang and I have to battle this serpent. Aang's distracting it. If I just bend the water into ice, everyone can just walk across the ice to the other side! It's working, but now I have to help Aang. I can't let him battle the monster alone! Take that! WHOOSH! And that! THWACK! Aang is spinning that way. I'll spin the other way until the monster is so dizzy he—BOOM!

He knocked right into the rocks, and now he's going back where he came from!

Just when I thought things had settled down, Ying's baby decided to come! I used to help my Gran Gran deliver lots of babies back home, so it's up to me to take charge. "Aang, get some rags. Sokka, water. Toph, I need you to make an earth tent—a big one."

Toph raised a large stone tent.

"Suki, come with me."

A short while later, Ying and her husband, Tahn, were the proud parents of a baby girl. I stepped outside the tent and found Aang sitting there with his head buried in his hands.

"Aang, you have to come see this," I said, pulling him into the tent.

Look at him, staring at the baby. Oh, gosh, he's crying! He's feeling something again.

"I've been going through a really hard time lately. But you've made me hopeful again."

"Hope," Ying said. "That's what we will name our baby."

"I thought I was trying to be strong, but I was really just running away from my feelings," Aang told me. "Seeing this family together, so full of love, reminded me how I feel about Appa. And how I feel about you."

That's so sweet of him! I knew he'd bounce back. Now he's off to try to find Appa in Ba Sing Se. We're going to go straight to the king. I'm sure we'll meet up with him really soon. Off he goes! Suki is leaving too. Sokka must be sad.

We are finally here—Ba Sing Se's outer gate. It's time to find the Earth King.

Chapter 7

58 What's Aang doing back here so soon? He was only gone for a few minutes. "I thought you were looking for Appa."

"I was. But something stopped me— something big."

What does that mean? Where's he taking us? Oh, no! There's a huge drill on the other side of Ba Sing Se's outer wall; it's moving toward the city! It looks like that thing is going to try to drill right through the wall!

It looks like those Earthbenders were try- ing to stop the drill, but failed. And one of the soldiers is hurt.

I manipulated the water from my pouch in a Waterbending healing move. Hmm. This is odd. He doesn't seem to have any physical injury. Yet he can't move.

"His chi is blocked," the general told me.

I can use a Waterbending healing technique to open up his chi paths again. There. That should be better. Good, he can move his arm again. "Who did this to you?"

"Two girls ambushed us. One of them hit me with a bunch of quick jabs, and suddenly I couldn't Earthbend and I could barely move. Then she cartwheeled away!"

"It's that girl—I think her name is Ty Lee!" She attacked me in Omashu along with Princess Azula. She punched me with those quick jabs and my bending vanished. It's a horrible feeling of weakness. I don't ever want to feel that helpless again. "She doesn't look dangerous, but she knows the human body and its weak points. It's like she takes you down from the inside."

Why is Sokka suddenly squealing and jumping up and down like a monkey? Sometimes he's so strange. "Yes?" I asked Sokka.

"What you just said! That's how we're going

to take down that drill. The same way Ty Lee took down all these big Earthbenders!"

"By hitting its pressure points!" Toph added, getting Sokka's idea immediately.

That's my brother. He's our plan guy. Just when I think he's gone over the deep end, he bounces right back!

"We'll take it down from the inside!" Aang said. "Sokka's plan has got to work. Everyone inside that wall—the whole world, in fact—is counting on us."

 He's right. I try hard not to spend every moment worrying about the fate of the world, and how it basically rests with our every action and choice, but it's the truth.

Sokka's plan worked! After weakening the drill's supports from the inside, Aang slammed the outside of the drill with a huge rock, stopping it in its tracks. I can't believe we did it! We stopped the drill and saved the city. Now we can finally head toward the Earth King.

We rode the train past the inner wall and got our first glimpse of Ba Sing Se. When we got out at the station, Aang pulled out his bison whistle and blew. "I'm coming for you, buddy."

Now that the distraction of stopping the drill has passed, Aang's had time to think about Appa again. I can feel his mood sinking. I've got to help keep his spirits up.

"He's here, Katara. I can feel it."

"We'll find him, Aang. I know it."

We've just been approached by a woman named Joo Dee. She says she's going to show us around. So strange. I wonder how she knew we were coming. She even knows all our names and she knows that Aang is the Avatar.

"Shall we get started?" Joo Dee asked.

"Yes," Sokka replied. "We have information about the Fire Nation Army that we need to deliver to the Earth King right away."

"Great!" she said. "Let's begin our tour."

"Maybe you missed what I told you," Sokka said. "We need to talk to the king about the war. It's important."

"You're in Ba Sing Se now," Joo Dee replied. "Everyone is safe here."

She's not even listening to Sokka. What is going on here? I know Aang and Toph don't like this place. I think that soon I'll understand exactly why. . . . In the meantime, I guess I should pay attention to the tour. I might learn something important.

So this is the lower ring of the city. It's a walled-off area where all the poor people and refugees live. It's so sad! It's like they're prisoners here in their own city. Here's the middle ring—filled with shops, restaurants, and Ba Sing Se University. This looks a lot more livable than the first ring.

"We have information that is absolutely crucial for the king to hear," Sokka repeated.

"Look, here's one of the oldest buildings in the middle ring, Town Hall," Joo Dee replied.

"Is that woman deaf?" Sokka asked.

"She hears you. It's called being handled," Toph explained. "Get used to it."

Joo Dee is definitely ignoring Sokka. But why? The fate of the world is in our hands. We have to get this message to the king!

"What's inside that oval wall?" I asked as we entered the upper ring.

"And who are those mean-looking guys in robes?" Sokka added.

"Inside the oval is the royal palace of the

king," Joo Dee explained. "Those men are agents of the Dai Li, the Cultural Authority of Ba Sing Se. They are the guardians of all our traditions."

"Can we see the king now?" Aang asked.

Good question! How can she say no to the Avatar?

"Oh, no," Joo Dee replied. "One doesn't just pop in on the king."

Unbelievable! But he's the AVATAR!

Now we're stopping. Why are we stopping?

"Here we are, your new home," Joo Dee said. Then she turned to talk to a messenger who just arrived. "More good news. Your request to see the king has been processed and should be put through in about a month."

A month? Every day we wait is one day less we have to plan our invasion of the Fire Nation. How could it possibly take that long for the Avatar to see the king? Aang shouldn't have to wait for anyone!

"If we're going to be here for a month, we should spend it looking for Appa," Aang said.

He's right. At least we can make good use of the time.

After a whole afternoon of searching for Appa with Joo Dee, who insisted on coming along, we came home without having had any luck. At least Joo Dee is finally gone! Not only isn't she helpful, but she seems to be intentionally blocking or controlling all our efforts to see the king and find Appa. And Sokka tried to ask our next—door neighbor, Pong, about the war. He told Sokka never to mention the war again, and to stay away from the Dai Li. I couldn't believe my ears!

"This is ridiculous," I said. "No one will talk about anything important. It's like there's a conspiracy."

"We have to find a way to see the Earth King," Sokka said. "That's the only way to straighten this out."

The next morning as I was reading the news—paper, it hit me! The king is having a party at the palace tonight for his pet bear, so we can sneak in to see him!

Toph and I are getting dressed up in fancy dresses, to try to blend in with the society

crowd. Earlier today she gave me some lessons on how to act like a rich society lady.
She knows all about that; her family is really
wealthy. It's actually kind of fun pretending
to be one of these women. Sometimes I think
about how different my life would be if my
parents were well-off, like Toph's, or even if
my grandmother had stayed at the North Pole
instead of migrating south. . . . It would be kind
of nice to be able to dress like this all the time. I
can't wait to see the look on Aang's face when
he sees me in this fancy getup—it's nothing like
my usual robes. I wonder what he'll say. . . .

"Wow! You look beautiful!" Aang said
immediately.

Beautiful? Oh my gosh, he's actually blushing! Wait, I think I am too. . . . Okay, Katara,
it's not such a big deal. So he thinks you look
beautiful, so what? It's just the excitement over
being a normal girl, that's all. It'll wear off. . . .

We're finally in the party and able to start
searching out the king. We almost got turned
away at the king's door because we didn't
have an invitation. (I guess the Beifong seal

of the flying boar doesn't work everywhere.) Then I saw this guy walking toward us and I told him my blind cousin lost our invitation—Toph must have loved that! Anyway, the guy, Long Feng, said he'd be honored to help us. Apparently he's the cultural minister to the king. I guess there are a few nice people here! Unfortunately he was also very protective—he kept saying he wasn't going to leave us alone until we found our families! Thankfully, Aang and Sokka snuck in on their own dressed as busboys.

"What are you doing here?" called a familiar voice.

It's Joo Dee!

"You have to leave immediately, or we'll all be in terrible trouble!"

What does that mean? How much damage could we cause? Oh, no—why is Aang Airbending! We're supposed to be undercover. Now everyone knows the Avatar is here! Wait, it looks like it's okay. Aang is going to entertain them while we look for the king. Okay, where could he be? Oh, there he is! And Aang's making his way over to talk to him. Finally! He's—wait, what's happening? Someone's grabbing me—AHHH! I'm being dragged out of the ballroom! What is this? Where are we, in some kind of library? Thank goodness, Sokka, Toph, and Momo are here. But where's Aang?

The door's opening. It's Aang and that guy who helped us, Long Feng!

"Why won't you let us talk to the king?" Sokka asked. "We have information that could defeat the Fire Nation!"

"The Earth King has no time to get involved with political squabbles and the day-to-day minutia of military activities," Long Feng replied.

No wonder he helped us in—we just made it easier for him to trap us!

"What's most important to His Royal Majesty is maintaining the cultural heritage of Ba Sing Se. It's my job to oversee the rest of the city's resources, including the military."

So that's it, then. The Dai Li, and this guy in particular, actually run things. No wonder we can't see the king. We'd find out that he has no real power here. This is what everyone's been hiding from us.

"So the king is just a figurehead."

"He's your puppet!" Toph added.

"Oh, no, no," Long Feng insisted. "He just can't sully his hands with the hourly changes of an endless war."

Finally, someone here admits there's ACTUALLY a war!

"But we've found out about a solar eclipse that will leave the Fire Nation defenseless! You could lead an invasion—"

"No!" Long Feng shouted. "It is the strict policy of Ba Sing Se that the war not be mentioned within the walls. Constant news of an escalating war would throw the citizens into a state of panic."

This is insane! The war is going to reach this city eventually. In fact it already has—we just stopped a huge drill from breaking through the outer wall! We didn't think Omashu would ever fall, but it did. Nowhere is safe from the Fire Nation. Not even Ba Sing Se. And believe me, they'll have more than their fair share of panic if they just sit back and do nothing.

"You can't keep the truth from all these

people! They have to know!" I cried out.

"I'll tell them!" Aang shouted. "I'll make sure everyone knows!"

"Until now you have been treated as honored guests," Long Feng said calmly. "But from now on you will be watched by the Dai Li. If you mention the war, you will be expelled from the city. I understand you've been looking for your bison. It would be a shame if you were not able to complete your quest."

He's threatening us! He knows we're searching for Appa, and he's threatening to kick us out of the city before we've had a chance to find him. Could it be that he even knows where Appa is, and is holding him prisoner to keep us quiet?

"Now Joo Dee will show you home," Long Feng said.

Who's that? That's not Joo Dee. . . .

"Come with me, please," she said, smiling.

"What happened to Joo Dee?"

"I'm Joo Dee. I'll be your host as long as you're in our wonderful city."

She's Joo Dee too? That's impossible. . . .

Chapter 8

We're trying to make the most of our time here while we're waiting to see the king, and that means finding Appa. Hopefully these missing—bison posters and fliers will help. Aang has been flying over the city spreading them every—where.

Someone's knocking at the door. It's Joo Dee—the first Joo Dee.

"What happened to you?" Sokka asked. "Did the Dai Li throw you in jail?"

"Of course not," Joo Dee replied. "I simply took a short vacation to Lake Laogai, out in the country."

That's odd. "But why did they replace you with some other woman who also said her name was Joo Dee?"

"I'm Joo Dee."

Yeah, lady, I heard you, but that still doesn't answer my question. Why am I even expecting an answer? She's ignored almost every question we've asked her since we got here. Boy, this conspiracy runs really deep. It's like it's compromised everybody. . . .

"I'm here to tell you that dropping fliers and putting up posters is forbidden."

"We don't care about your rules!" Aang shouted. "We're finding Appa on our own, so just stay out of our way!" Then he slammed the door in Joo Dee's face.

I guess we're not following their rules anymore. Finally! I mean, usually I think it's best to try to work things out before it gets to this point, but that clearly isn't happening here. These people will do anything to stop us from speaking the truth, even if that means keeping us from Appa. We were never going to get any help from Joo Dee or the Dai Li.

We're heading out with piles of

missing—bison posters. If we split up, we'll cover more ground. . . . I'll go this way.

"Katara?"

HUH? I know that voice. It can't be!

"I think I can help you."

I don't believe it! Jet! Here in Ba Sing Se! I'm still so mad at him for flooding that village, I could scream! Since he's so fond of floods, I'll show him a flood. WHOOSH!

"Katara, I've changed!" he cried as the powerful rush of water slammed him into the alley's back wall.

"Tell it to some other girl, Jet!" I can never trust him again. Never! I cared for him, really cared for him. I thought he was brave and strong and good. And then he failed me.

"I don't want to fight you!" he yelled, slash—ing my ice daggers with his sword.

What's he doing? He's dropping his sword to the ground. But wait, what's he reaching for? I knew he was lying!

WHOOSH! It's not so easy to fight when you're pinned against the wall with ice dag—gers, is it, Jet?

"Katara, what is it?"

Sokka! Thank goodness. "Jet's back, and we can't trust anything he says."

"But we don't even know why he's here," Sokka said.

"I don't care why he's here. Whatever the reason is, it can't be good." Why is Sokka defending him? He knows what Jet did!

"I'm here to help you find Appa," Jet said.

Huh? What's that rolled up in his hand? It's one of our Appa fliers. I thought he was reaching for a weapon. . . . Well, I don't want his help. I don't want anything to do with him!

"Katara, we have to give him a chance," Aang said, catching up to us.

"Katara, I swear I've changed," Jet pleaded. "I was a troubled person. I let my anger get out of control. But I don't even have my gang now. I've put all that behind me."

Talk is cheap. All that talk about saving innocent people from the Fire Nation and doing the right thing, and yet he flooded an entire village just to prove a point! Well, I'm not going to let him do this again. He's not going to make me trust him. "You're lying!" What's Toph doing? She's walking over. She's feeling the wall he's leaning against. Is she going to take out the wall?

"He's not lying," Toph announced. "I can feel his breathing and heartbeat. When people lie, there's a physical indication. He's telling the truth."

"Katara, we don't have any leads," Aang added. "If Jet says he can help us find Appa, we have to check it out."

So nobody feels like I do? They're all willing to just forget about what Jet did and believe him. Maybe I'm overreacting. Why am I still so mad at him? I guess I can't ask Aang to pass up any opportunity to find Appa just because my feelings for Jet are . . . complicated. "All right. But we're not letting you out of our sight."

As we followed Jet to the warehouse where he'd heard they were keeping Appa, I tried to make sense of my feelings. Maybe it's just been a really long time since I've had someone to lean on, someone who was older, someone who was wise and brave. I guess that when I met Jet, I was so excited because he was kind of that person to me. He was totally devoted to fighting the Fire Nation; I didn't even have to convince him of how important it is! And I guess I did sort of feel a special connection with him. I felt safe when he was around, and then he betrayed that, he betrayed ME. I'd really like to believe that he's changed, but what if he hasn't? What if I get hurt again?

Time to snap out of it—we're here. . . . So Jet WAS telling the truth. Appa was here, but the janitor said that he's been sold to some guy who took him to some distant island. Maybe I can trust him again after all. . . .

"I don't care how far it is," Aang said. "We have to try."

Aang's right. Now that we know where Appa is, we've got to go after him.

"All right," Sokka said. "Let's get moving."

"I'll come with you," Jet said.

"We don't need your help." I already have way too much to deal with. I can't handle him, too.

"Why won't you trust me?" Jet pleaded.

He can't be serious, can he? How can he ask that question? "Gee . . . I wonder."

"Was this guy your boyfriend or some—thing?" Toph asked.

What? Why would she ask that? She wasn't

even with us when everything first happened—
how does she know that we weren't just friends?
Am I acting like an angry ex–girlfriend? Is that
why she said that? "No!"

"I can tell you're lying," Toph said.

She's infuriating.

"Jet!" someone called out.

It's those two kids from his gang. I knew it! I
knew he was lying! He's never going to change,
and I almost fell back into trusting him.

"I thought you said you didn't have your
gang anymore."

76

"I don't," Jet said.

He has some nerve to continue to lie right
to my face when the proof that he's lying is
standing right here.

"How did you get away from the Dai Li?"
one of his gang buddies asked.

"The Dai Li?!" Is he in with those thugs too?
What if this really is a trap?

"I don't know what you're talking about,"
Jet said.

"He got arrested by the Dai Li a few weeks
ago."

"This doesn't make any sense," Toph said,

feeling the ground between the two of them. "They're both telling the truth."

"That's impossible." Jet's lying, I just know it.

"No, it's not," Sokka said. "They both think they're telling the truth. Jet's been brain-washed!"

What? So he is being honest after all? Wait a minute—if that's true, things are starting to make sense. . . .

"The Dai Li must have sent Jet to mislead us, and that janitor was part of the plot too."

"We need to find a way to jog Jet's real memories," Aang said.

"Maybe this will help," I said, bending the water from my pouch into a band around Jet's head. Hopefully my healing abilities will cut through the brainwashing.

"They took me to a headquarters under the water," Jet recalled. "Like a lake."

"Wait!" Sokka said. "Joo Dee said she went on vacation to Lake Laogai."

"That's it!" Jet cried. "Lake Laogai!"

We went to Lake Laogai, where Toph dis-covered a hidden tunnel leading down to the

Dai Li's secret headquarters under the lake.

Jet's leading us down a hallway toward the cell where he said they were holding Appa. Now, that's really strange. There's a roomful of women all practicing to be Joo Dee! No wonder that new Joo Dee just ignored my question and acted like she'd been with us from the start—the Dai Li brainwashes them! This place is even creepier than we thought.

"I think it's through here," Jet said, stopping at a big door and flinging it open.

Long Feng! And a squad of Dai Li agents! It WAS a trap. Jet double-crossed us—again! I can't believe I let this happen!

"Take them into custody!" Long Feng ordered, and his Dai Li began fighting us.

What? It looks like Jet is fighting on our side—against the Dai Li! I can't figure him out, I'm so confused! But now I have to focus my energies on the Dai Li. I'll deal with Jet later.

"Long Feng is escaping!" Aang cried. Then he and Jet took off after Long Feng while Sokka, Toph, Jet's gang, and I finished off the rest of the Dai Li agents. When we found Aang and Jet, Jet was sprawled out on the ground. Oh, no, he's hurt! It looks really bad. I can't believe that I was so cruel to him, and he really was just trying to help.

Wait! Maybe I can heal him. Okay, here it goes. . . . He should be up and walking any min— It's not working. Why isn't it working? "This isn't good."

"You guys go find Appa, we'll stay with Jet," his friends said.

"We're not going to leave him." I can't leave him, not now, not like this. He needs to get better. I need to find a way to make him better.

"Don't worry, Katara," Jet said with a smile. "I'll be fine."

His smile, it's so sweet. I can't believe this happened. . . . I guess this is good-bye.

Okay, Katara, just stay focused on finding Appa. . . . We're almost at the other cell. Whatever you do, don't think about Jet.

"He's gone!" Aang cried, busting open the empty cell. "Long Feng beat us here."

We dashed back up the tunnel and out to the lake's shore, but found ourselves surrounded by Dai Li. They raised high stone walls.

We're trapped. We'll never get to tell the Earth King about the eclipse or invading the Fire Nation. And poor Aang. My heart is breaking for him. . . . Appa is gone! Now he'll never find him—wait, why is Momo going so crazy, screeching and jumping and flying into the air? What does he see?

It's Appa! Appa's flying toward us!

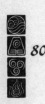

After Appa helped us take out the Dai Li, he flew us to an island in the middle of the lake where we could all rest. Aang is so relieved and happy, it's wonderful to see. But we didn't rest for long. At first I wanted to just leave this place behind us, but Sokka convinced us that Long Feng can't threaten us anymore because we have Appa! Our chances of getting the information to the Earth King are much better this time around!

So we battled our way into the palace.

Finally, we're in the throne room! The king is surrounded by guards, some Dai Li agents, and Long Feng himself.

"Detain the assailants," Long Feng ordered his agents. "Make sure the Avatar and his friends never see daylight again."

"You're the Avatar?" the king asked.

The king agreed to come with us to Lake Laogai. Now we can prove to him that Long Feng and the Dai Li have been plotting to overthrow him! Finally, we're making progress. We just need to get to the lake—

Something's wrong. Where's the tunnel that leads down under the lake?

"The tunnel is gone," Toph announced. "There's nothing down there anymore."

The Dai Li destroyed the evidence. They've covered everything up!

"Long Feng was right," the king said. "This was a waste of time. I'm going back to the palace."

We can't let it end here. We know the truth, but it doesn't matter if we can't convince the king. There's got to be something else to prove that—wait! That's it. "The outer wall! They'll never be able to cover that up in time!"

Please be there, please be—THERE! "It's still there."

"What is that?" the king asked, surprised.

"It's a giant drill," Sokka explained. "Made

by the Fire Nation to break through your walls."

"I can't believe I never knew," the king said, obviously shaken by this discovery.

"I can explain this, Your Majesty."

Long Feng! How's that snake going to slither out of this one?

"It's nothing more than a construction proj—ect," Long Feng said.

"Oh, really? Then perhaps you could explain why there's a Fire Nation insignia on your construction project." Take that, you nut!

"Dai Li, arrest Long Feng!" the king

ordered.

Yes! Finally, he believes us. Now we can actually do something with the information we have about the eclipse.

"I thought my people lived in peace," he said. "But it was an illusion."

"That's why we came here, Your Highness," Sokka said. "Because we think you can help us end the war."

"We don't have much time," Aang explained. "There's a comet coming this summer. It will give the Firebenders unbelievable strength. They'll be unstoppable."

"But there is hope," Sokka continued. "A solar eclipse is coming. The sun will be entirely blocked by the moon, and the Firebenders will be helpless. That's the day we need your army to invade the Fire Nation."

"Very well," said the king. "You have my support."

This is what we've been waiting to hear for so long. Finally, things might be okay.

That's when General How, leader of the Council of Generals, arrived with some amazing news. "We've searched Long Feng's office. There are secret files on everyone in Ba Sing Se, including you kids."

Toph got a letter from her mom saying she wanted to see her. Aang got a scroll from a guru; he's waiting for Aang at the Eastern Air Temple. He says he can teach Aang how to control the Avatar state!

"Here is an intelligence report," the general said, handing me some papers.

"A small fleet of Water Tribe ships are protecting the mouth of Chameleon Bay. They are led by Hakoda! Sokka, it's Dad!"

Gosh, I've missed him so much. I worry about

him every day. I've kept up hope, but it's easy to get discouraged. . . . Sometimes I even get angry with him, for leaving us behind. There have been so many times when we needed his help, so many moments when I wish he was here with us. And now we are actually going to see him!

"I hate to say it, but we have to split up."

"Split up?" Aang protested. "But we just found Appa and got back together."

"Aang, you have to meet this guru so you'll be ready to invade the Fire Nation. Toph, you need to see your mom."

"I guess you're right, Katara," Aang said. "I could drop you and Sokka off at Chameleon Bay so you can see your dad."

"Someone has to stay here with the Earth King and help him plan for the invasion," Sokka said. "I guess that's me."

Gosh, I'd love to see Dad. But Sokka needs this more than I do. He's been waiting for years for Dad to come back so they can go into battle together, so Dad can be proud of him. I can't deny him the chance. "No, Sokka. You go to Chameleon Bay.

I'll stay here with the king."

I've never seen Sokka so happy—overwhelmed with emotion is more like it. Now he's giving me a big hug. "You are the nicest sister ever!"

I know, Sokka. I know.

I'm really going to miss these guys. They've become family, complete with all the love and all the arguments.

"Katara, I need to tell you something," Aang said as he loaded his stuff onto Appa. "I've been wanting to say it for a long time."

"What is it, Aang?" Hmm, he's been wanting to tell me for a long time? But we're always together. This feels like a big deal. He looks so nervous. He's blushing . . . and we're all alone. Oh my gosh, is he going to tell me he loves me? I've thought about it, lots of times. . . . What will I say? I mean, I love Aang as a . . . as a—

"Katara, I—"

"All right!" Sokka interrupted. "Who's ready for a little men-only man trip?" He punched Aang in the arm playfully.

SOKKA! He ruined it! Then again, maybe Aang wasn't going to say anything romantic at all. Who knows? I mean, yes, he told me I looked beautiful when I got dressed up for the Earth King's party, and in the Cave of Two Lovers he—this is crazy! He probably just wanted to say he was going to miss me. Either way, I wish he had the chance to say whatever it was that he'd been waiting so long for. I wonder how long it will be before the moment comes back again. . . . Now he's turning away—he looks so deflated! "Wait, Aang."

Here's a hug, and a kiss—on the cheek. There'll be time to talk, when he returns.

As the king was wishing us luck, a royal messenger arrived.

"Your Majesty, there are three female warriors from Kyoshi Island here to see you," the messenger announced.

"That's Suki!" Sokka exclaimed.

"Do you know these warriors?" the king asked.

"They are skilled warriors. Trustworthy, too. And they're good friends of ours," Sokka said.

"Then welcome them as honored guests," the king ordered.

Safe travels, my friends. I'll see you soon.

Chapter 9

Today Momo and I are joining the generals for a strategy meeting about the invasion.

"General Fong's base will serve as the launching point for the attack," General How announced. "In exactly two months, the army and navy will invade the Fire Nation, on the day of the solar eclipse. All we need is the Earth King's seal in order to execute the plan."

We've talked about this invasion ever since we left the library. Now it's finally becoming a reality. We finally have a plan to end this war.

"I'll get these scrolls to the king right away," I volunteered, picking up the scrolls.

"Thank you very much, General How."

Look at that beautiful tea shop! It looks new.

"What do you say, Momo? A cup of tea before we get back to the palace?" It will give me some time to relax and catch my breath.

"Table for two, please." Strange . . . that waiter looks familiar. But I've never been in here before.

"Uncle, I need two jasmine, one green, and one lychee," the waiter called out.

Uncle? That voice is familiar too. But it can't be.

"I'm brewing as fast as I can!" shouted back the man near the kitchen.

It IS him. It's them—Zuko and Iroh, here in Ba Sing Se. They're posing as tea makers. But this means that the Fire Nation HAS infiltrated the city. I can't let them see me. I've got to warn the king that the city and all of our plans are now in grave danger!

I raced back to the palace as fast as I could run and dashed into the king's throne room.

Oh, the Kyoshi warriors are here. "Thank goodness you're here, Suki. Something terrible is going on. The Fire Nation has infiltrated the city. I just saw Prince Zuko and his uncle! We have to tell the Earth King right away!"

"Don't worry," Suki said, stepping out from the shadows. "I'll be sure to let him know."

Wait a minute. That's not Suki! I know that voice. It's Princess Azula under all that Kyoshi warrior makeup! First Zuko, now Azula. What did she do to the real Kyoshi warriors? I hope Suki is all right. This is horrible. The whole city is infested with Fire Nation. Everything's going wrong. I have to stop them now! I'll create a quick water whip and—no!

Ty Lee is too fast. She somersaulted out of nowhere and jabbed my shoulder. Losing bending. I can't control the water. It's splash-ing all over the floor. Ohhh . . . can't move, falling down . . . my chi . . . it's blocked!

They're all just staring down at me. I'm so helpless . . . and so is Ba Sing Se! Oh, Aang, I wish you were here. . . .

"So, Zu-Zu's in the city too," Azula cackled. "I think it's time for a family reunion."

Azula didn't know that Zuko was here? I thought they were acting together . . . but now she's going to team up with him. There's no one else in the city who knows they're here. There's no one to stop them and I can't move!

They're dragging me to an underground prison; it looks like a series of caverns beneath the city. "Let me go!" It's no use. No one can hear me down here, and no one knows where I am. I've never felt so helpless in my life!

I've got no sense of time down here. Azula and Zuko could have gained control of the city already. I—what's that? The door in the ceiling is opening.

"You've got company."

It's a Dai Li agent—he's throwing someone down the ramp. No . . . I don't believe it. Zuko! A prisoner just like me. I'd laugh if I wasn't so angry.

"Why did they throw you in here? Wait, let me guess. It's a trap, so that when Aang shows up to help me, you can finally have him in your little Fire Nation clutches."

He's just staring at me not saying a word. Now he's looking away, trying to ignore me. Well, I'm not about to let him do that.

"You're a terrible person, you know that? Always hunting the Avatar, trying to capture the world's last hope for peace. But what do you care? You're the Fire Lord's son. Spreading violence and hatred is in your blood."

"You don't know what you're talking about."

What? Now he finally decides to speak and he accuses me of not knowing what I'm talking about! Boy, is he arrogant. "How dare you. You have no idea what this war has put me through. Me personally. The Fire Nation took my mother away from me!"

Oh, no. . . . Please don't cry, Katara, not in front of him. . . .

"I'm sorry," Zuko said softly. "That's something we have in common."

Us, having something in common? What does he mean? His own people took his mother away too? But how is that possible? She's the Fire Lord's wife.

But what if he is telling the truth? What if Azula really is his enemy too? She did blast Iroh that time in the deserted city and even called Zuko a traitor. Maybe I have it all wrong, like I did with Jet. I was so hard on

Jet and now I regret it. Do I want to make the same mistake all over again? Still, it's so hard to trust the person who has come to represent the Fire Nation to me for so long. But we could be stuck down here together for a long time. Maybe I should give him a chance, but take things slowly. "I'm sorry I yelled at you before."

"It doesn't matter," Zuko replied.

"It's just that for so long now, whenever I would imagine the face of the enemy, it was your face."

"My face. I see."

He's reaching for his scar— "No, no. That's not what I meant." I could never be so cruel. I never thought the Fire Prince would be so self-conscious.

"It's okay. I used to think this scar marked me—the mark of the banished prince, cursed to chase the Avatar forever. But lately I've realized that I'm free to determine my own destiny—even if I'll never be free of my mark."

Hmmm . . . maybe I can make a first gesture in uniting us against Azula. He seems like he might be rethinking his purpose. Maybe I can get him to come over to our side if I just show him he can be forgiven. Maybe if he felt that he could actually be part of a family who loved him, things would be different. . . .

"Maybe you could be free of it. I have healing abilities. And I have this. It's water from the Spirit Oasis at the North Pole. It has special properties, so I've been saving it for something important. I don't know if it will work, but . . ."

He's letting me touch his scar without backing away. Maybe, just maybe, this will—

THOOM! The wall, it just caved in!

"Aang!" He's found me! I've never been happier to see him! "I knew you would come." And Iroh is with him. Maybe they ARE on our side now.

"Uncle, what are you doing with the Avatar?" Zuko asked.

"Saving you, that's what," Aang replied.

Zuko's moving toward Aang! I thought he said he was done doing the Fire Nation's dirty work. Oh, why do I keep getting let down by these people? I thought I was a good judge of character, so why do I keep getting it all wrong? And I was ready to heal him. . . .

"Zuko, it's time we talked," Iroh said. "Aang,

go help your friends. We'll catch up with you."

Aang and I ran through the cave until we came to a huge crystal cavern.

"I don't know what to do, Katara. Everything's just out of control this time. I have a bad feeling we're too late to stop Azula."

"We'll take it one step at a time, Aang. First we have to find Sokka and Toph."

THOOM! What is that? It's Azula—she's attacking us! She is truly powerful, but Aang and I can do this. Good has to outlast evil—it just has to! Okay, we're gaining on her. She's losing speed against the both of us. . . .

FOOM!

Where'd that come from? That wasn't Azula—it was Zuko! He's joining the battle. But whose side is he on? He's staring at Azula, now back at Aang. His help could turn the tide of battle. Maybe he is going to change; maybe our conversation did help him see the light. . . . Oh, please, Zuko, do the right thing—

THOOM! No! He's shooting a fire at Aang! I should have known better than to even think about trusting him! Again, I allowed myself to be fooled into thinking that he is good at heart. "I thought you had changed!"

"I HAVE changed!"

Oh, boy, here come the Dai Li, and they're helping Azula! We can't fight Zuko, Azula, and the Dai Li all on our own. . . .

What's Aang doing? He's creating a crystal tent all around him. Now he's going into the Avatar state and rising from the tent in a column of energy. Hopefully everything he learned with the guru will come in handy; they don't stand a chance against the Avatar—

NO! Azula! She blasted Aang with light-ning! It pierced his tent! He's tumbling to the ground. WHOOOSH! Take that, Dai Li! I've got to catch him before he—got him! But he's not moving . . . and now that I have him, how will we get out of here?

Another Firebending blast? It's Iroh!

"You've go to get out of here!" Iroh shouted at me. "I'll hold them off as long as I can."

He's the only honest Firebender I've ever met. I only hope I get to thank him someday. . . .

I managed to escape with Aang and reconnect

with Toph, Sokka, and the Earth King. We're finally flying away from Ba Sing Se.

I have to heal Aang. I've been saving the water from the Spirit Oasis for something important. That time has come. I can't believe I almost used it on Zuko! I'm furious with myself for trusting him. What was I thinking? I only hope I can actually heal Aang. I can't lose him. I can't—wait, he's stirring! He's breathing. He's alive! He looks weak, but at least he's smiling at me. He's going to be all right. But what about the rest of us, and the Earth Kingdom, and the whole world? Are we going to be all right?

"The Earth Kingdom has fallen," the king announced, staring down at his beloved city.

I thought we were going to fix it all. I thought, despite everything we had to endure, that we would succeed. But I was wrong. And now we're in exile. The whole world is under Fire Nation command. It's okay, Katara. Just take a deep breath and concentrate on Aang. One step at a time, remember? Now is not the time to lose faith, not when we've depended on it for so long. Never lose hope. We will defeat them. I truly believe that Aang can save the world.